Purple!

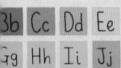
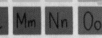

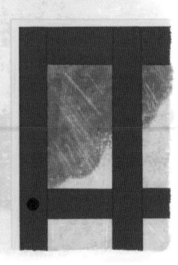

Some of the children in the preschool were painting. They were doing some colour mixing.

"I've just seen that blue and red makes purple!" said Poncho, watching the painting.

Kodi had a look, "Now they're mixing red and yellow, It makes orange!" Kodi growled excitedly.

Zingy had a look next "Yellow and blue is making green!" said Zingy.

"All the colours are making brown now!" said Poncho, swishing his cape around.

Gigi and her friends were watching all that was going on.

Some of her doll friends were being bathed in water and bubbles.

'Pop pop pop.' the children would say!

It was almost 8 o'clock and the children would soon be arriving for breakfast.

The hard working nursery staff Jen and Josie were already seeing the children in. Some children were happy, some children were feeling sad to be leaving their mummies or daddies.

Gentle encouragement and cuddles from Jen and Josie made the children feel better, and the children settled and ate their breakfast with their friends.

This is Kodi the soft brown teddy bear. Kodi is feeling excited to start the day.

This is Poncho who is a wise llama. He wears a hat and cape like a wizard. Poncho is proud of his hat and cape.

This is Zingy. Zingy is a zebra with rainbow stripes. She stretched her four legs and was happy to start the day.

"Rise and shine, it's a new day!" Said Gigi the Dolly softly.

This is Gigi. She has purple woollen hair, a soft face and wore a pinafore dress.

About the Author

Hi I'm Holly.

I have spent over 10 years working in early years. I love reading stories to the children and this inspired me to write my own stories. I hope it inspires your children's curiosity and imagination.

Reading stories to your children from a young age really helps their language development, it can also help with their bed time routine.

Any activities or children in the story are purely fictional for your entertainment.

Dream House Adventures

Bubbles and Fun

Orange

Green!

Brown!

Zingy the zebra had been taken off the shelf. One of the children in toddler's was upset. Zingy the zebra liked cuddles. After her friend felt better Zingy got put back on the shelf. "What was the matter with little Eva?" Gigi asked Zingy. "One of the other children took a toy away from Eva." explained Zingy.

"Oh no, that's not nice!" said Poncho. "It made Eva sad to have the toy taken away." Zingy told the other toys. "Yes, but sharing toys can be really hard to do when you're little so the other child might be sad too." Gigi said wisely. "That's true, Laura the nursery nurse from toddlers helped. She explained to Eva's friend it wasn't nice to snatch and helped her make the right choice to give the toy back. The other child soon found a different toy to play with and everyone felt happy again." Zingy told the other toys. "I'm glad my cuddle helped little Eva." Zingy said jumping excitedly.

It was the end of the day and the children had gone home. "It's been a busy day at Dream house." said Zingy.

"What shall we do now that the children and nursery nurses have gone?" Gigi asked her friends.

What do you think they're going to get up to?

Write your thoughts here...

Printed in Great Britain
by Amazon